MW00890393

For Sophie

With special thanks to
Megan Tingley and Mary Gruetzke

First Edition

Library of Congress Cataloging-in-Publication Data

Landry, Leo.
Oh, baby! / by Leo Landry. — 1st ed.
p. cm.
Summary: Illustrations and simple text, including several nursery rhyme verses, provide an unusual look at the world of babies.
ISBN 0-316-60732-0
[1. Babies — Fiction.] I. Title.
PZ7.L2317357 Bab 2003
[E] — dc21 2001050202

10 9 8 7 6 5 4 3 2 1

TWP

Printed in Singapore

The illustrations for this book were done in watercolor and pencil.
The text was set in Providence, and the display type is Schneidler.

LEO LANDRY

Oh, Baby!

A Celebration of Babies

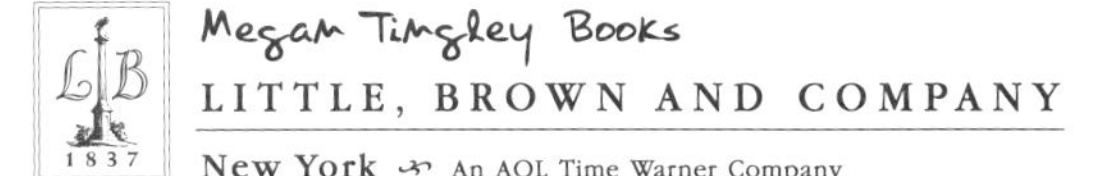
LB 1837
Megan Tingley Books
LITTLE, BROWN AND COMPANY
New York — An AOL Time Warner Company

Baby Food

We love banana baby
a whole bunch.

Baby peas peek out of pods.

Baby and I were baked in a pie,
The gravy was wonderful hot.
We had nothing to pay to the baker that day,
And so we crept out of the pot.

Egg baby cracks up.

Happy birthday, baby cakes!

This little baby is the apple of my eye.

Popsicle babies are cool.

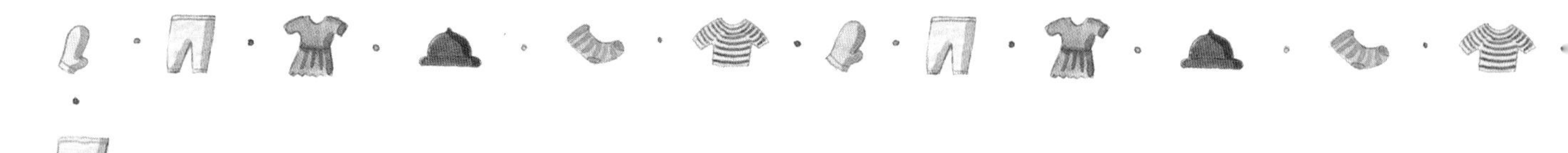

Baby Clothes

Sock it to me, sock babies!

"Let it snow,"
says snowsuit baby.

Pocket baby comes along
for the ride.

These babies are
short and sweet.

Diddle, diddle, dumpling, my son John,
Went to bed with his trousers on.
One shoe off and one shoe on,
Diddle, diddle, dumpling, my son John.

Mitten baby
needs a helping hand.

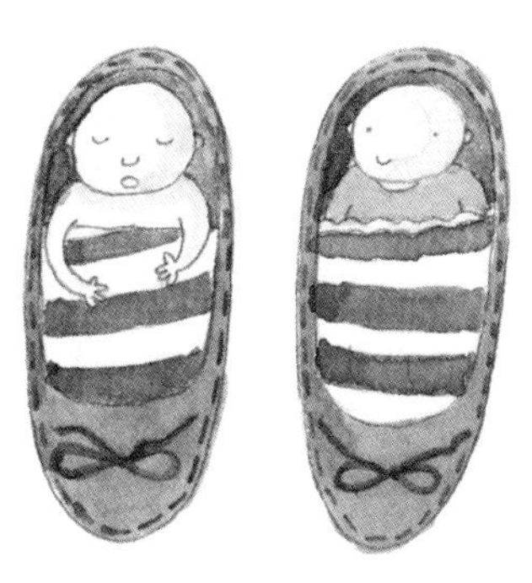

Sleep tight, slipper babies.

Nature Babies

Bee babies buzz by.

Seashell baby hears the ocean.

Dandelion baby makes a wish.

Leaf baby blows in the wind.

Starfish baby stays on the shore.

Acorn baby drops in.

Rain, rain, go away,
Come again another day,
Little baby wants to play.

This baby is
getting down to business.

Mailbox babies deliver good news.

Robber baby steals your heart.

Cowgirl baby rounds 'em up.

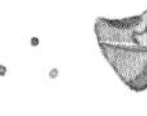

Construction babies go on a big dig.

Police baby is on the beat.

I've been working on the railroad
All the livelong day,
I've been working on the railroad
Just to pass the time away.

Baby Animals
Stork baby
makes a special delivery.
Hop along, kangaroo baby.
Kitten baby takes a catnap.

Piggy baby takes a mud bath.

Possum baby hangs around.

Little Robin Redbreast
Came to visit me.
This is what he whistled,
"Thank you for my tea."

Wolf baby howls at the moon.

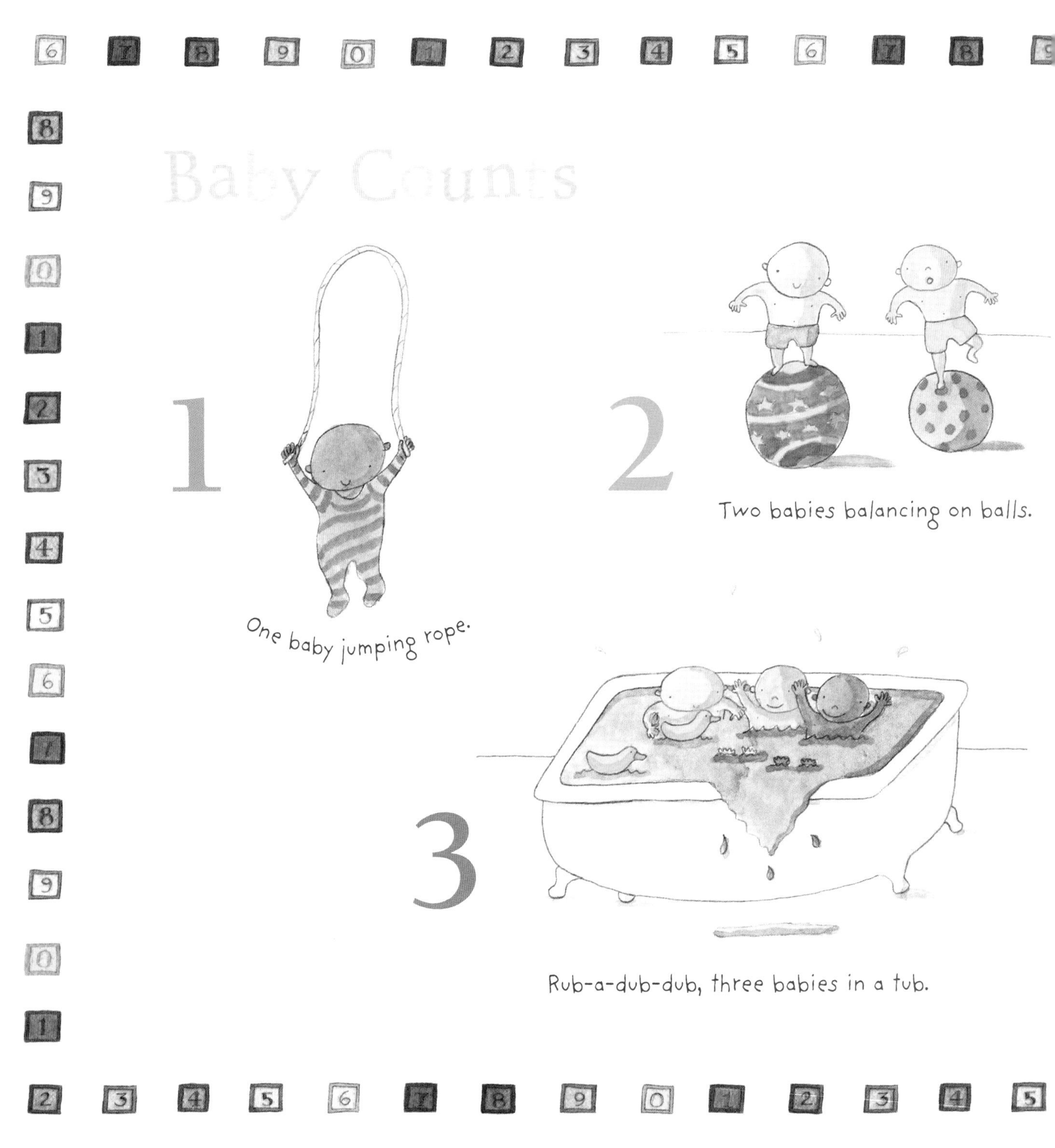
Baby Counts
1
One baby jumping rope.
2
Two babies balancing on balls.
3
Rub-a-dub-dub, three babies in a tub.

4

Four musical babies bang and clang.

5

Where are the baby mice? Squeak, squeak, squeak.
I cannot see them. Peek, peek, peek.
Here they come from the hole in the wall,
One, two, three, four, five—that's all!

Baby Plays

Balloon babies are sky-high.

Baby makes a basket!

Roller babies go for a ride.

"I see you!" says peekaboo baby.

Fly away, airplane babies.

Dance, little baby, dance up high!
Never mind, baby, Mother is by.
Crow and caper, caper and crow,
There little baby, there you go!

Swing, baby, swing!

Fairy Tale Babies

Up, up, up climbs beanstalk baby.

"Just right," says Goldilocks baby.

Aladdin baby makes a wish.

Little Baby Riding Hood
Went a-walking in the wood
On her way to Grandma's house
She's as quiet as a mouse.

Cinderella baby goes to the ball.

Rapunzel baby waits
in her tower.

Noisy Babies

Rock 'n' roll babies sing, "Yeah, yeah, yeah!"

Fussy baby cries, "Boo, hoo!"

Piano babies play a tune.

If you're happy and you know it,
Clap your hands.
If you're happy and you know it,
Clap your hands.

Bongo babies bang a beat.

la la la

Chatty baby talks baby talk.

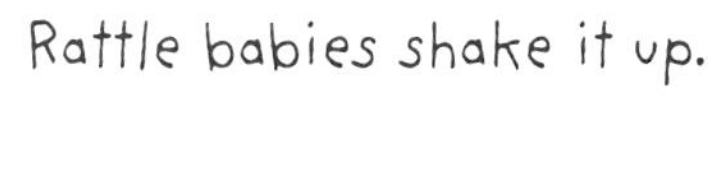

Rattle babies shake it up.

Baby Toys

Hello, dolly!

"Quack, quack!" says duck baby.

Ring around a baby!

Block baby is busy building.

Here's a ball for baby,
Big and soft and round;
Here is baby's hammer,
See how he can pound!

Bucket babies
go to the beach.

Baby gives a bear hug.

Baby Colors

Little Boy Blue, come blow your horn.
The sheep's in the meadow,
The cow's in the corn.

Flower baby sits pretty in pink.

Baby loves fire-engine red.

Yellow sun shines on beach baby.

Artist baby paints with purple.

Orange is pumpkin baby's favorite color.

Spring baby plays in the green, green grass.

Baby Bedtime

Splish splash baby takes a bath.

Twinkle, twinkle, little star,
How I wonder what you are!
Up above the world so high,
Like a diamond in the sky.

Sleep tight, blanket babies.

Baby bat stays up late.

Mobile babies
float off to sleep.

Bedtime baby crawls in her crib.

Book baby reads herself to sleep.

Leo Landry

has been a bookseller at an independent children's bookstore for seventeen years. He lives with his wife and daughter in North Easton, Massachusetts.